COUNTRY MUSIC

ZANE KOSS

INVISIBLE PUBLISHING
Halifax | Fredericton | Picton

"*Country Music* is both delicate and ferocious, tender and steely. Known for his conceptual flair, translation practice, and complex poetics of location, Koss here shows he has even more strings to his bow—including a tale-telling brio as he stakes his claim to a poetry of common life. A book humming with attachment and grief and rage and humour, *Country Music* offers teen hijinks and misdemeanours, grim encounters with cougars and coyotes, a family's rich tradition of storying their (and others') lives. *Country Music* is both a homecoming and a complex measuring of the distance from home—from a working-class childhood in Western Canada, a community anchored in jobs in mining and logging and mills, a life rich in dirt roads, skidoos, hunting, biking, hard labour, shared meals, and shared jokes. Koss maps an emotional vista and landscape; the book emerges as an effort of self-location, a deep connection sought and sustained amid the pandemic spent in Brooklyn. Family stories and friends' fates are lovingly, complexly summoned and channelled as Koss undertakes a sounding and a grounding. Spackled with violence, hilarity, grotesquerie, these poems are animated by Koss's profound listening and attentiveness and a kind of wild longing. These are poems as if exchanged among friends and family, as if generated around an archaic campfire, as if John Prine had spent his youth in the Kootenays, as if poetry were still a medium of common life: and suddenly we see with this book that it is."

MAUREEN MCLANE, author of *My Poets*

"The voices we've heard linger in our memory and imagination, tangled in the stories we continually tell ourselves about ourselves. A poem is a useful way of connecting our own voice into this entanglement. In *Country Music* Zane Koss does this by decomposing the anecdotal within the mycelium of family, community, and the land. His exploratory poetic intervention into memory and the local allows him to locate his voices and make up his own story. As he says, 'I wanted to write a poem that would somehow place me.'"

FRED WAH, author of *Music at the Heart of Thinking*

Library and Archives Canada Cataloguing in Publication
Title: Country music / Zane Koss.
Names: Koss, Zane, author.
Identifiers: Canadiana 20240501047
ISBN 9781778430633 (softcover)
Subjects: LCGFT: Poetry.
Classification: LCC PS8621.O86 C68 2025 | DDC C811/.6—dc23

Edited by ryan fitzpatrick and Kate McKenna
Cover design by Megan Fildes
Interior design by Megan Fildes
Typeset in Laurentian
With thanks to type designer Rod McDonald

Invisible Publishing is committed to protecting our natural environment. As part of our efforts, both the cover and interior of this book are printed on acid-free 100% post-consumer recycled fibres.

Printed and bound in Canada.

Invisible Publishing | Halifax, Fredericton, & Picton
www.invisiblepublishing.com

Published with the generous assistance of the Canada Council for the Arts, the Ontario Arts Council, and the Government of Canada.

Canada Council for the Arts Conseil des Arts du Canada
ONTARIO ARTS COUNCIL
CONSEIL DES ARTS DE L'ONTARIO
an Ontario government agency
un organisme du gouvernement de l'Ontario
Canada

for
grandpa,
beetle, farmer,
and mom

Turn wheresoe'er we would, he was a light
Unfailing: not a Hamlet could we pass,
Rarely a House, which did not yield to him
Remembrances; or from his tongue call forth
Some way-beguiling tale.

— William Wordsworth

You old fucking prick, I was hoping you'd died already.

— Traditional, East Kootenays

We all use language, we talk with it, we do various things with it; surely the one place that poetry can just take off from must be the very beginnings of the individual's entrance into language.

— Robert Duncan, on Charles Olson

Gee, really, I guess I'm too much of a story-teller. I don't mind if we never read another poem, I'd like to finish this story.

— Charles Olson, Berkeley lecture

tell the cougar story

so jerry and tom go out

this one time to check jerry's traps he's got a line out

for lynx and you have to check these quite regularly

so the poor thing isn't stuck there so long that it starves

to death or chews its leg off to get out it's just

a regular foot trap staked to the ground

and they get there to where it's supposed to be

and it's gone but there's some tracks heading out

over the snow, big tracks, not a lynx and they follow the tracks

and there it's this huge cougar the trap stuck on its paw

dragging the chain and stake and jerry's only got his 22

because he'd thought it would just be the lynx

and so he's firing shots at this thing's head

and they're just ricocheting off the slope of the cougar's skull

and so jerry says to tom, now tom i've got

the other gun in the back seat of the truck

pats his breast pocket says i've got the only two bullets for it

right here just grab the gun and hurry back

so as tom leaves the cougar starts to make a run for it,

so jerry and the dog follow it along and corner it

somewhat again,

and the cougar starts lunging at jerry

and jerry's just got the empty 22 he'd unloaded the full clip

dinging off its skull and so he's swinging the rifle at the cougar

like a baseball bat and it's lunging at him

and every time it lunges the dog bites at its ass

and jerry's swinging at the cougar and eventually it figures out

somehow that it can swing the stake and chain that it's got

attached to its paw so it's swinging this chain and charging

and tom's gone to get the gun to finish it off

and jerry can hear the truck door creak open

and close again and he thinks finally he's got it,

then the truck door opens and closes

and then the other side again and eventually

tom comes hustling back down the trail and says

i've got the gun but i couldn't find any bullets

looked all over and jerry says you dumb sonofabitch

i've got them right here in my goddamn pocket

and so he puts one in and the cougar gets wise

and takes off just then so the shot misses

and they have to run it down again

and finally get there, line it up last shot

last bullet and finally boom put the poor fucking thing out

no not that one, though that was quite the story

oh really, no? not quite sure what one you mean

i mean the one

isn't there one where your dad

oh fuck

that one

so my mom called me completely in tears disintegrating

and i thought

oh shit, grandma's died

and she starts talking thru the tears, saying

billy's dead, a cougar got him

and i'm relieved that it's just the cat but my mom

loved that cat like none other and she's saying

he didn't come in at bedtime

so i was laying there awake all night waiting

if maybe he'd come by the window and call to be let in

and i'm laying there

and i hear him come pounding up onto the deck in a panic

and something else pounding up the stairs after him

so i think one of the neighbourhood cats

must be bullying him again so i go to let him in and get out

on the deck and he's at the far end and i can't see

what's happening so i turn on the light and it's this

ginger-coloured dog laying on its side and i'm thinking

what the heck is it doing there then i see billy's

little orange tail sticking out from where its face would be

and it's got him and it's clutching him and kicking

at his body and holding him there so i scream and it turns

and looks at me and i don't know where it comes from

deep inside of me seeing that cougar's face turn and stare

back at me like cavemen or something chilled me

absolutely to my bones and i ran back inside screaming

and crying saying a cougar's got billy a cougar's got billy

and your dad comes running out of the bedroom

and of course he's still naked and runs down

to the basement to the gun cabinet to grab a gun

and he's loading it as he comes back up and runs out

onto the deck and the cougar's alarmed by the commotion

and so it's standing now and holding billy in its mouth and

of course your dad can't shoot because it's back on

the far side and mclellan's place is just beyond

and we don't know if they're home or not

so he grabs one of the deck chairs

and starts fighting the cougar with it

and he can tell by now the way billy is hanging limp

in the cougar's mouth that he's already dead but

your father he's a good man and i love him

he wants to get billy's body back for me

so we can bury him and say goodbye

and so he starts swinging the deck chair at the cougar

and trying to get it to drop billy and it's trying to get away

with its prize i'm sure it's hungry and worked hard

for this meal but he sees your dad swinging this deck chair

at him and must have calculated his chances

and drops billy and runs past your dad and down the stairs

and we pick up billy and he's dead

sobbing, breaking the narrative with exhausted sobs

and my dad apparently on the other line listening, says

i should have shot that bastard when i had the chance

so yes, that's it

i'm shocked by it all and my heart is breaking for

my mom because of how much she loved that cat

but i'm just picturing my dad buck naked on the deck

with his gun, swinging a deck chair at a cougar to

reclaim the corpse of his wife's beloved cat

he's a hero

and i feel terrible but i'm on

the phone just trying to hold it all together and

y'know, i hadn't fully absorbed the death

just the shock of the crazy story

first thing in the morning just trying so hard not to laugh

because of the whole scene my mom had

yeah

trying to hold it together tears flooding my eyes

yeah, that was the one

that was the one i wanted to hear

in the back
    forty
I walk the dog,
                        dead now
and watch the stars.
Years later,
after moving away,
I purchase glasses
and put them on
when I drive home from the bar.
The stars
become
so much m
       ore vivid but
the dog still dies.

sometimes
we stand in the weeds and howl

at the
coyotes
they ghost
in the hidden corners
of the field
watching us build

we bark like dogs
and they dis
appear
into the long
grass

sometimes
they would kill our cats

seen that picture of you
with the gun

  with the twelve-gauge pump-action
  shotgun
and the dead birds, pixelated

while you mourn your grand
father; i bet you   are wondering;

        but me,
i never shot anything except
popcans and paper targets,
but i know it,   clubbed
fish to eat; gutted
      them,   myself

  one time my dad brought
home a tiny rabbit
  in a cardboard box   that
his skidder had disturbed

we looked in
at it, then   let it go back
      in the woods; that sense
of wonder, seeing something

so different,   alive in your
hands;
                   where have our fathers
gone i have still lived more years
of my life

                         on a dirt road than a
paved one,
i tell people that, and

  though   true, it doesn't
                   feel that way; mike,
       where have we gone

let's get a trapline, and some
traps; an old skidoo;   on a winter
night, we'll get back to the truck
from a long day   and

stop at someone's winter camp
on the way home;
            we will steal their wine,
 and i will trick you   into eating
the dogs' food you'll be so drunk
it will be easy; soaking wet, you

will have to curl up on the
                floor on the passenger
side, to get close to the   heater,
and pass out;   i will drag you green
      up your front
steps, and into your trailer; theresa

relieved that you are not dead,
will threaten to kill us   both, and
together we will strip you naked and put you

in the warm bath;   you will hurt, for
      days afterward, and take years
before you can go down the dog food aisle
          trust me, it will make
a good story;

mike, send me a poem, that
you've written, in .docx format
and i will return,

*

I wanted to write a poem

that would somehow

place me

late night

kitchen table

stories

a campfire

All my sense

depends upon

that

the beer bottles
mark time   gathered around, telling new
ones   the old ones saying tell that one about the
time you come down off mclean lake on the dirt
bike uneven surface of the varnished wood where
leaves have been added to expand the social body
is the voices gathered around that table   in the dark
or what about that time jimmy flipped his truck out
westside road   this is all i ever wanted to   (be
gathered around the kitchen table   it seems so
small   in the dark a voice and cascading
laughter   it was everything that ever needed   to exist
i want to delete facebook   i don't want to
delete facebook   so i can send a pdf to mike
ask him to send me his most recent poem   to be
back around that kitchen table   ask
jerry what's that one about that time   or
tell me that one about   the strip mining of
data from our lives   about blowing up the creek
with dynamite for gold panning about the buildings
storing our photographs in data servers   fragments
of rock falling around their heads as they ran   what about
our lives have we lost   what about that time
you went out to ralph lake with tom   tell me
about the time you put all the rocks in his sleeping bag
oh fuck that bastard was mad as hell   i can only
look at these places on google maps now   can hardly
write this poem without it spiralling into another and
another   and another place   another story   the palliser
middle fork of the white   diana lake   these
exist as words i can see on a screen   not the frigid water
where i got soaked to the thighs   dragged up the trail

by an orange loop of binder twine tied to my father
or gathered   the words i have been gathered
around this kitchen table
                                                             to hear these words

knew he was a logger
drove skidder

had not considered

never asked

until
a friend from out east, ontario,

asking

had told friends, he built pretty well all the roads
in the backcountry

knew 'em

had built them, so that others could clear cut whole blocks

regenerating, thick with trees as tall as i

until asked

and my dad, then, telling

it's never a great sign when you're skidding the logs down to the landing and they pass you on the slope
—get ready to jump, never wore a seatbelt for that, jump quicker
oh yeah, few times

a wife, two kids at home

don't ever get in a bar fight with a chain man, eight hours a day dragging a hundred pounds of chains up and down the mountain side, beat the shit out of you like you were nothing

had never bothered to ask

scraping a living out of the bush
dragging the trees
                                        down to the landing

i watch, each summer, on social media, as the poets from
Toronto and Montreal arrive in the mountains
for the prestigious residency

discover nature, scraping a living from the bush
dragging words from each scenic vista, extracting content
                                                                                value

                                                        sent east on rail lines

I wanted to write a poem that would mend the

guilt I feel the first cool days every autumn,

smelling two-stroke from

leaf-blowers, as if two-stroke chainsaw exhaust, the cool

of the air on my face, that same sensation out getting

firewood for the winter. That I should be there
helping, each year.

That I should be there

the landscape

of my childhood does not mother poems

no mer, lapping waves

rhythmic eternal

no watery womb to emerge from

nor a kinetic city of motion

a linkage of bodies

the landscape of my imaginary

dense thickets of willow

that give way to clogged creeks

of logjams where we would fish

and i would get wet to the thighs

parallel firs that grow into walls

or open into tangled slidepaths

dry branches that whipped your eyes

so you could not see the mountains

until you left home and returned

A poem I could never write.

A poem I wrote every single fall since I left home.

Had always been afraid of storms
                                                  they told me
                                    I,
                                                who had known her last
my grandmother—scratch it:
Baba.
                              My baba.

In a hospital bed unable—
Had known her tall in the kitchen arguing
in Ukrainian with Gido,
                                    whose name had shifted from
                                    the prairie to the mountains

Had always been afraid of storms
would call down, from the top of the gulch
whenever the wind picked up across

Not always, had been

                              a child

Had been a child milking a cow,
struck dead by lightning
her hands still on the warm udders
the milk curdled in the pail.

Trembling in her hospital bed the wind

Began like this.

Kate asks me,
when are you going to stop identifying as blue-collar

you will probably never work with
your body ever again in your life

I said,

when i stop feeling like

now most summers the smoke drifts across the continent

the exact grey-orange sky i grew up under

and i can breathe it in

    can’t breathe in it

there is a war going on in my hometown

at the centre of town, the cenotaph

in my head in my heart

i read the reports each morning

that come to me on social media

i am on the other side of a continent

sheltering in place

wondering what stake i have in home

i contribute nothing and read stories

friends type into their phones

assaulted by white supremacists

what is my relation to place

except except except

my father
had taken me
behind the cardboard screen
age five

to pick a candidate
from a list of names
saying *you choose one. it doesn't matter*

years later, red in the face
saying *you can't tear history down*
the drive home from the airport

an inexplicable anger

no longer someone i understood

while now
mom, on the phone,

saying *he*
wants to put a Black Lives Matter
sign at the end of the driveway

still inscrutable these changes
viewed from the other edge of the continent

how these things have happened
why i wasn't

there
to understand them

or am not now

hiked two hours up to the treeline
to find the lake frozen
fishing rods in hand

standing on the ice
shotgun barrel against the surface:

BOOM

is that enough of a fucking ice fishing hole for you?

BOOM, BOOM

that big enough for you?

This poem, I write each night in my head, when I can't sleep.

Forget the words by morning. How I've memorized

every story I

ever

*

and mom saying

so i guess that's what she'd tried to do, to go down the next row, to visit her parents there, not thinking that it was like two feet of snow, and of course they'd only cleared that little area, and so she takes one step into the snow, picture this five-foot-tall seventy-five-year-old Ukrainian woman, and she takes one step and immediately sinks into the snow and loses her footing, twisting around and lands on her back, in the three feet of snow, and i see it happen in slow motion, but what can i do, and the poor kid working the crank sees it too and goes over to help, but she's not exactly nimble, and stuck on her back like a goddamn turtle, and she's thrashing about trying, trying to get herself up, pauses, settles a moment, so she can get up again, and the kid is trying to grab her and hoist her out but she's not making it easy, thrashing around, and finally her son turns around and sees her, and he just goes "ma! what the heck are you doing?" like she's decided that this would be the perfect time to make snow angels, thrashing around, stuck on her back, making snow angels, and he's going "ma!" just like that "ma! ma! what are you doing?" [almost in tears laughing] *and so him and the kid together, finally one grabbing each arm, hoist her up, up, out of the snow and back onto the cleared part, and the kid finally turns around, and we make eye contact, and i'm trying so hard not to laugh, and he's trying so hard not to laugh, and he just kneels down at the crank there, and starts lowering the coffin into the ground, his whole body just shaking, trying so hard, because it would be awful, of course, but just beet red, shaking, crying,*

cranking the coffin
down into the ground,

her son still going "ma! what were you doing?"

telling the story with her whole body

arms flailing, the twist and slip, face shifting between

as if re-living
as if it came up out of the ground   her body the conduit

always knowing how to draw it out thru the repetitions

baroque, cycling back thru, fractal details, tension

and release

always the sly winking

falsely dumb, playing

the funny-man fool to

the straight-man dupe

laughing,

grinning

a wink

*

I think about performance

how to perform a poem how

reading these words to an   audience

could replicate that social context

gathered round the kitchen table

telling the old stories, improvising

within a structure

tell that one about

that time you and jerry

how to put that on the page

how the page could be the space

in which that social field is made

visible   improvising against each others'

that's like this one time, we

how to make the page the space

where that happens

alone

the page the context in which improvisation   could

driven by the difference only

                    only possible in otherness

to make the page a space of

confronting my own otherness to myself

as a means of improvisation

cannot quite

am the subject delineated by that context

there was a patch of black ice there
at the sixteen kilometre
and one of the boys'd radio'd up
a cow moose had slipped on it
was struggling
so i drove down
and see her struggling to stand
she's got her front legs up but can't
get the back ones
so i get behind her
tell her "okay, take it easy, now" an act of trust
and start trying to lift her up
so she can get her legs under her intimacy,
hands on her hips
and the boys are driving by, y'know
looks like well and she's looking back at me
and moaning
she realizes i'm trying to help
but it's clear her hip broke in the fall

he put

a bullet
in the back of her head
and dragged her body into the ditch

an act

of kindness

intimacy
what
are we to learn by this
what gained in the telling
repeated?
that we are so close to death

the humour, too,

appearing to fuck a moose

while the boys drive by in loaded trucks

her moaning, that moment of

eye contact

we are within the animal world
and must make kindness where
we can

must take, not take, must

place our own bodies back into the earth

why keep telling

these

stories

why i would give anything
to hear them again

and

again

and

the shadow of an airplane passes over the apartment

i am in brooklyn

in a pandemic

*

so it was the week before Halloween
and there'd been this black bear spotted around town
eating garbage a dog or cat had gone missing
and the neighbour come over to say
she was worried
what with all the kids going around
in the dark
in costumes
who knows what could happen

and i was doing yard work the next day
and there it was walking down the street
so i ran inside and grabbed three apples off the kitchen counter
put 'em in my pocket
and loaded a couple slugs into the shotgun

so i toss an apple out in the front yard
and it runs over and gobbles it up
and i toss an apple into the side yard
and it runs over and gobbles it up
and i go back thru the house out the back door
and toss an apple up against the woodpile

i put the barrel of the shotgun
behind its ear
and pulled the trigger

went inside and called the cops and CO to tell 'em i shot
a bear out of season without a tag
and discharged a firearm within town limits

come and get me

the telling is repetition

whose story to tell

who is the i who intrudes in each

could i be

spent years punishing myself

for not

have not lived up to

drunk at a party

arms flailing, telling another another

wanting that connection
                                        telling another

always
                someone else's

and so:

truck flipped upside-down

resting on its cab in the middle of the road

twenty miles out from town

into the bush

and there we are with our lighters

trying to read the scrapes the truck left

in the hard-packed dirt

to figure out which way

to walk the twenty miles

back into town

reading the signs of the accident,

scratched across the hardened surface

or:

i looked at him and said

i told you you dumb sonuvabitch

i've got the bullets in my goddamn

or:

built like a minifridge with arms

as wide as tall neck disappearing with the years

his dad half-blind with drink driving

the truck into the propane tank

at shift's end each friday

cut off a finger to buy him a snowmobile

with the settlement amount

picked an appendage to match exactly

that

am now scraping

extracting

myself from

he was the last one out
off the cut block
and they reckoned
later
his truck must have broke down
and he figured
to walk the ten kilometres
back out
to the highway, hitch a ride
they could follow his footsteps
in the dust along the edge of the road
[################]

[###############################]
[#########################]
[###]

[###################]

[########]

and that was all they found

who gets to tell this story or
more important
who gets to hear it

where do i fit in the chain of
                                        responsibility for carrying this story
                                        this life, this
                                        [######]

i have heard it
what responsibility do i now carry

                                        and you

well, and how the fuck could you say no to her

big blue eyes, age six

looking up at you and saying

daddy i just wish you wouldn't

kill packrats in the cabin with the shotgun

while we're sleeping

it's too loud

this poem is an elegy

what do i make   with words

after a kilometre or two

grizzly tracks started following on top of his
a couple hundred yards further along
he carefully placed his lunchbox on the ground beside his tracks

another few feet he placed

his hard hat

and that was all they found

my canon comprised of works like

you old fucking prick, i was hoping you'd died already

old swiss carpenter hearing

hammered thin by decades of saw

and drill *what's that what's that*

all laughing all laughing crying

what's he fucking say what?

oh sorry i'm a little early, but you know me, it's in my nature

well you can fuck right off then cuz it's in my nature

oh, you know me, i'm an easy-going guy

bullshit

never been in a single fight in my life
bullshit

except that one

blind drunk, stealing hubcaps
off the cars lined up at the
swimming hole screaming *go fuck yrself*
until someone chased him
running down the highway and
beat the shit
out of him

and that other one i guess
though it wasn't much of a fight

fucking bastard deserved that one though

smashing a wine glass across his face at the pizzeria

"for the country will bring us no peace"

cannot now raise his arm above his shoulder
cannot now, forty years at the mine

retreating into himself

if, in 1972, a new snowmobile cost $_____
if, in 1972, you worked at the mill
if, in 1972, your son wanted a new snowmobile
if, in 1972, the union at the mill had negotiated
    standard compensation rates for common injuries at the mill
if, in 1972, that rate was $_____ for a finger
                                        —or more, for a thumb, and scaled by the
knuckle—
if, in 1972, your finger was cut off at work, precise to the knuckle,
and the next month your son had a new snowmobile
how many days since the last workplace incident

how many days would you hit the propane tank in the yard
with your truck as you rolled home from the mill after work
beer bottles clattering between the gas and brake, how many days

if, in 1972, your house had not yet running water
and you had to run to the pipe in the yard had
to run to the outhouse, how many rolling stones
albums had been released what gadgets in the car
james bond then drove what the avant-garde publishing in 1972
where a CIA-sponsored coup imposing
democracy a green revolution presidential
wiretapping what hydroelectric what nuclear power plants
                                                                                    came online

if, in 1977, you, drunk, flipped your truck 20 miles out
the westside road, and you and jimmy by the flame
of your two lighters trying to read the hieroglyphs of
the hard-packed dirt road to determine which direction
was 20 miles walk back into town and which a thousand further
into the pitch-black bush

if, in 1982, you came upon the upturned truck of
your friends' father, and pulled a little German man out
of the wreck with three roofing nails stuck into the bald patch
on the top of his head, and when he went to grab
the still spinning wheel of the truck to stall out the motor
and was instead sucked into the wheel-well and pinned
against the inner fender—you, holding back the laughter—how
many days since

if, in 1992, your son cried when you strung up the carcass of a
deer in the shivering garage

how many days
since

at the grad student pub
the grad student whose
aunt had that famous
french theorist over for dinner parties is telling a story

and so we're like in west virginia or something
and we pull up to this gas station

and the guy pumping our gas is like missing a finger
and we go in to pay

and the woman's like missing a tooth
and we're like we need to get out of here

before something happens to us

wordless I left the bar blind with an anger I still feel
a decade later
still feel

I tell people this story now

it's a good story

or, at least

it says something

what could happen to us

and so kim's got her fishing rod out
to whack anyone that starts to get ahead of her
as we run back around the lake to the cabin

taking pot shots

across the lake at the
grizzly

totally fucking unfazed

that fall, over the col, in the next valley

would stalk and kill
two moose
hunters, the third only

made it back to the truck alive

shots ringing around it
from the other shore

when they tell these stories now

i fill in the lost details

as they try to tell them

wanting it exactly

as i remember it

every rhythm

every detail

these days hand-feeds the cats scraps from the table;
but sometimes, the urge overcomes me, to lay my hot
coffee spoon against the thinnest skin on the back of
kate's hand; it comes up deep from below, faster than i
know how to fight it; when i tell her you used to do that
to me at the breakfast table, every morning, she can't imagine
you thus.

truthfully, i can no longer either

stumbling teenaged six a.m.
out of bed for the big hike
these two men who love each other
one to the other at the door
oh, i'm a bit early, but,
you know me, it's in my nature
and my dad to him:
well, you can fuck right off then
cuz it's in my nature
this love and how
his baseball-glove head
inflates up, purple and crinkling
at the eyes
grinning back to his
crooked canine
laughing hard, good.

my mom
tells me poems
over the phone
sometimes
when she calls

and they say things
like this

and he's dying of cancer
so i'm sure someone told him
by now
a doctor
but then he looked up at me
and asked
what does palliative mean
and what could i
say

or she tells me
which kindergarten classmate
overdosed
but mostly

when my mother calls me
she tells me about the cats
they
are doing fine, she says:
they are doing
fine

one time my neighbour had me get rid of the dog for them

while they were a week on vacation

brought the 30/30

it was a mean sonuvabitch

had to shoot from the hip

fucking thing almost ate me

blood all over the place

on their little concrete patio

fuck there was a lot of blood

why my desire to arrest this motion

to get the stories down just
right

as if possible

my first instinct
finding that i was
a writer

to preserve these

for what

    from what

so we thought we'd take our motorbikes
up to diana lake
because no one had done it before

about three quarters of the way up
we realize how bad an idea this was
on the way back down
i'm ahead of jimmy

and i wait on a corner, and he's gone
so go back up looking and
there's jimmy's bike up in a tree
below the bank

and jimmy's there hunched over this stump
and as i pull him off, this stick on the stump
had been stuck into his gut

and his shirt was just soaked in blood

so i lift it up there and look
and—bloop—out pops one loop of his intestine

so i grabbed a stick and poked it back in there
ripped my t-shirt into a strip and tied it around his gut
clamped his hand over it and said hold on tight

why place them onto the page

why circulate them beyond

what right to their own self-preservation

is

precisely

their resistance to

we get to the bottom there
and i say let me take another
look at it, bleeding had stopped and
—bloop—intestine pops out again

so i grabbed a stick
and poked it back in there again

i don't think he ever went to the hospital
we were too afraid to tell his parents

a social context that cannot be provided

here.

so i had this cow moose tag
and jimmy and i were gonna go up by whiteswan
and we had the radios from the mine
so we could take the dirt bike scouting
and we'd radio back to each other
if we saw anything

so i'm way up out [######] creek
and jimmy calls on the radio saying
"you better come down here quick
i just shot a cow moose in the campground"
so i go "whaddaya mean in the campground?"
and he says "just get down here quick"

so i get down there, and sure enough
he's shot a cow moose just there
in the turn-around at packrat point
and people are starting to gather

and just as i get there the ranger comes running over
just bawling

"what in the heck did you do that for?"
"we've got a cow moose tag"
"well, why did you shoot this one, it was the camp pet, it was practically tame!"

and jimmy goes
"well, i guess that's why it let me walk right up to it
and shoot it in the face"

there is an extractiveness
to these stories

never in relation to the land except
in opposition

an opposing force
that must be overcome

a relationship that is rooted
in a history

in a particular history

taking place

against

taking place

dynamiting the creek
the gold
vanished into the air

for a moment
the creek ceased to flow

fragments of rock falling

around their heads
as they ran

i held the quivering body of the cutthroat in my hands
for a heartbeat

thinking about the sound its skull would make being crushed
with a gnarled branch
                                        its muscles tensed with sensation

have done many times before
have done
before i slid it back into the water

                                                        and it vanished
                                                              in the current

what does it mean to tell these stories
against this,

        against

the land is
i am

how to hold onto one
without losing the other

how not to lose what relations
i am held by

that i hold

to hold accountable
without crushing

the bird's shivering ribcage
in my fingers

cannot touch without destroying

lit out down the gully
from the birthday party
and boys
fired slingshots at deer
just strange and sad
                        older now.

he said his dad put all three cats
(one for each brother)
into a cardboard box
and shot that box full of of. of
                        (fair's fair.)

of. and that it's still out there in the
shotg.unshells.   woods somewhere

am held by

the forest fires on the mountainside
visible from the kitchen window

my dad texts me photos daily
of the smoke rising over the job site

house under evacuation alert

i am on the other side of a continent

*

this one old timer, who put his longjohns on in october

and didn't take them off until march

they had to cut them away from his body

the hair had grown thru the fabric

the skin fused to it

this is not a story

this is all the stories

This is the only poem

I ever wanted to write

I wanted to tell you a story

I don’t want to have to write another poem

*

And the creek is up   /again
        silt creeping the wetlands
against the current

and i seen it later
                    from toby hill
                       (peter's hill
(restraining order
                    arrested, and
                    and silt sliding upstream
like a surface
                            hiding

the sandbar   from the bridge

               and below the bridge
                    where i'd walked two
weeks before   in the rain

               —

these are the things
that concern us

         and my head throbbing
                    since sunday,
                     father's day,
                     and today,

\

wild horses

used to be a herd up behind wilmer, one up steamboat

used to breed old studs in with 'em
let the old studs loose, inject some new blood, breed it into them

one time / palominos / down near canal flats

made beautiful
horses

small horses (bigger than rad's
(peruvian pasos

good saddle horses
tough feet
never fell
ride 'em anywhere, never fall

palominos

forestry
offered a reward one winter

three bucks, a pair of ears

or maybe they rounded up the mares and shipped them to the slaughterhouse

and shot the last few studs
they couldn't catch
maybe that was it

shot 'em

my dad used to say
he'd come up by where your place is now
and see carcasses everywhere.

that's what it was: a reward for a pair of ears.

shot 'em all, canal flats to brisco.
shot 'em all.

carcasses rotting

in the blood red

sunset

how they weave and touch and sprout
a shared organism

voices in the dark
and we laugh
we laugh until we are crying

and we are all crying

*

My brother

Began the story.

So it was the last morning

Began telling—

No.

No. Let your brother tell the story.

And I began.

It went like this:

I tell my friends that

my proudest moment, once

my brother, starting to tell a story

, my dad

interrupted to say, *No,*

let your brother tell it.

And so I told it

I wanted to write a poem

that would take me back home.

Because I could not be

that would be a home.

I wanted to tell you
a story.

SOURCES

All passages of italicized text, and some of the other passages, are direct quotations—as best I can remember—from the following people: Jerry Kohorst, Tom Statham, Larry Koss, Judy Koss, Kate McKenna, John Linstrom, and others that I'm forgetting. There are errors in my recounting of these stories throughout this book.

I want to thank each of these people for making me the person that I am, especially as a writer, and for their contributions to this book. It seems too obvious to say this book would not exist without their stories and their voices.

This book would not exist without their stories and their voices.

ACKNOWLEDGEMENTS

This book is for Jerry Kohorst, Tom Statham, Larry Koss, and Judy Koss. This book borrows their voices and tells their stories. Kate McKenna, John Linstrom, Jimmy Maione, Max Helmer, Rene Spoochi, and others make appearances, too. I am grateful to each of them for the role they've played in the creation of this book.

The stories in this book happened within the unceded territories of the Ktunaxa Nation and the Secwépemc people. This book was written on the traditional territories of the Munsee Lenape, Canarsee, Haudenosaunee, Kanien'kehá:ka, Anishinabe, Attiwonderonk, and Mississauga peoples.

Immense gratitude to ryan fitzpatrick for his vision and for being one of the strongest believers in this book. Mike Chaulk has been a tireless supporter of this project since the very first poems included in this volume were written, circa 2013.

Parts of this book have previously been published in *CV2*, *Poetry is Dead, the /temz/ Review, Touch the Donkey*, and as the Model Press chapbook *kitchen table*. Thank you to the editors of these publications.

Thank you to the whole crew at Invisible Publishing. Norm has been a constant cheerleader for this book. Thanks to Kimberley for guiding this book from manuscript to publication. I am always blown away by Megan's design work. Thank you to Jules for helping to get my books into readers' hands.

This was initially a difficult book for me to share with people, given how close it cuts to the bone. I am grateful for all the friends who shared their enthusiasm for this book at readings, private and public, especially MC Hyland, Andrew Gorin, Lytle Shaw, and James McDonald.

All my love and gratitude to Kate forever, who makes life possible and meaningful, and who has guided this project from its inception with her greater wisdom.

Invisible Publishing produces fine Canadian literature for those who enjoy such things. As an independent, not-for-profit publisher, we work to build communities that sustain and encourage engaging, literary, and current writing.

Invisible Publishing has been in operation for nearly two decades. We released our first fiction titles in the spring of 2007, and our catalogue has come to include works of graphic fiction and nonfiction, pop culture biographies, experimental poetry, and prose.

We are committed to publishing writers with diverse perspectives. In acknowledging historical and systemic barriers, and the limits of our existing catalogue, we emphatically encourage writers from LGBTQ2SIA+ communities, Indigenous writers, and writers of colour to submit their work.

Invisible Publishing is also home to the Bibliophonic series of music books and the Throwback series of CanLit reissues.